Little Princess

THIS BOOK BELONGS TO

_____

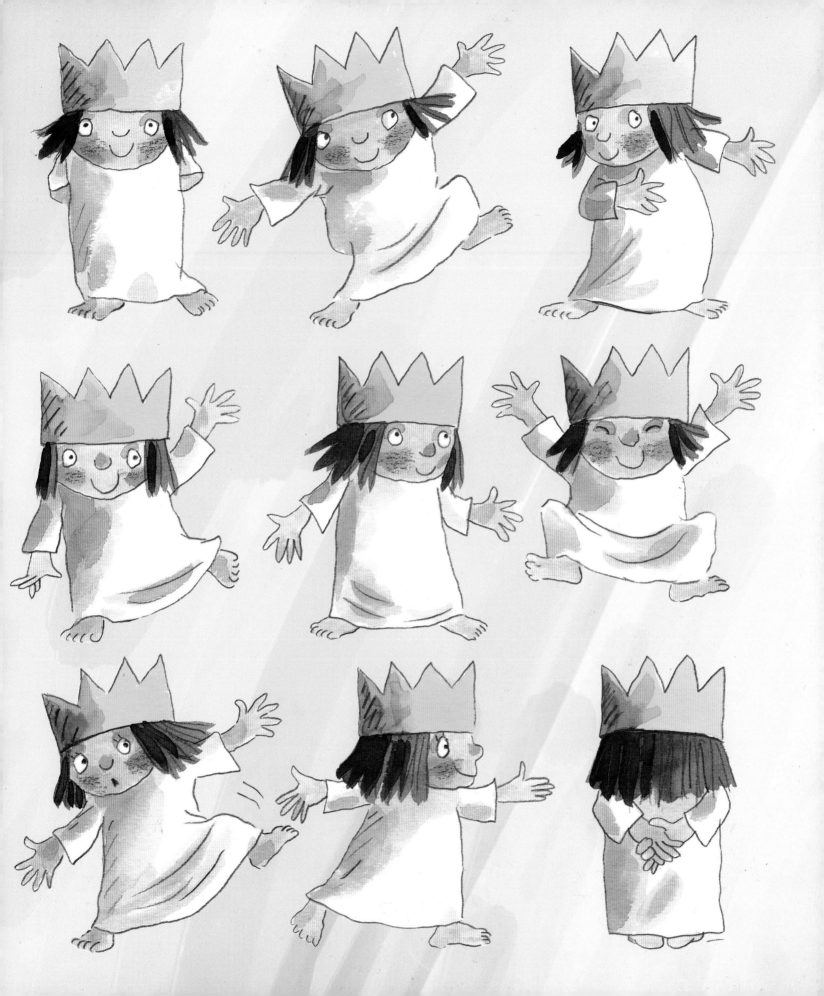

To Lara and Poppy – keep on reading!

This paperback edition first published in 2018 by Andersen Press Ltd.
First published in Great Britain in 2017 by
Andersen Press Ltd., 20 Vauxhall Bridge Road, London SW1V 2SA.
Copyright © Tony Ross, 2017.
The right of Tony Ross to be identified as the author and illustrator of this work
has been asserted by him in accordance with the Copyright, Designs and Patents Act, 1988.
All rights reserved. Colour separated in Switzerland by Photolitho AG, Zürich.
Printed and bound in China.

1   3   5   7   9   10   8   6   4   2

British Library Cataloguing in Publication Data available.

ISBN 978 1 78344 594 3

Little Princess

I Want Snow!

Tony Ross

Andersen Press

It was the summer holidays and the Little Princess
was having a picnic in the garden with the King.

The Queen was away counting penguins at the South Pole.
It was so nice at the South Pole that she sent a postcard home.

The postcard was of a snowman. "What's this white stuff?"
the Little Princess asked. "What does it DO?"

"Oh, that's SNOW," said the King. "You can build a snowman out of it and you can slide on it and have lots of fun."

"I WANT SNOW!" squealed the Little Princess. "I want to build a snowman and a snowcastle and a snowgilbert, and, and..."

"WHOA!" whoaed the King. "It's summer. It is too warm for snow. You only get snow in the winter, when the weather is COLD! But you can have fun in the sun too."

But the Little Princess didn't want to wait for the cold weather.
"I WANT SNOW NOW!" she screamed. So everyone in the castle
rushed about looking for snow in summer.

Of course, there wasn't any snow anywhere.
"Let's pretend then," said the Maid. "Let's get dressed up for snow."
"BRRRRR!" said the Little Princess and she put on her coat.

Then she put on her woolly hat, her woolly scarf,
her woolly gloves and her big snow boots. She was SO hot.
"I DON'T LIKE THE SUMMER!" she gasped. "I WANT SNOW!"

In the garden, the Prime Minister built her
a snowman, out of stones.

The Little Princess looked at it. "That's a rockman, not a snowman," she said. "I WANT SNOW!"

At the beach, the Admiral built her
a snowcastle out of sand.

The Little Princess jumped on it. "That's a sandcastle, not a snowcastle!" she snapped. "I WANT SNOW!"

"Let's have a snowball fight," said the General in the garden,
scooping up a handful of mud.

The mudball hit the Little Princess on the nose.
"That's not snow!" she said. "I WANT SOME SNOW."

As it was too sunny to find snow outdoors, the Little Princess set off to look in the castle. "It's always cold in the castle," she thought. "Perhaps I can find some snow there."

"I WANT SNOW!" she said to the Cook.
"You're in luck," said the Cook, "I do happen to have
some snow in this cupboard."

He handed over a tiny glass globe, with a tiny Princess inside.
He shook it, and tiny snow swirled about.
"Look," he said, "the princess has snow."

"POO!" said the Little Princess. "That's not real snow.
I WANT REAL SNOW! I'm going to go to bed for ever!"
she shouted, stamping upstairs. "Or at least until it snows."

And the Little Princess stayed in bed for ever, only getting up for her meals, and to play with her friends, and to go to school, and to watch a little TV.

One morning, the Little Princess looked out of her
bedroom window to see snow falling and
a blanket of white over the whole land.

She leaped out of bed, put on all of her woollies, and rushed out. Her friends all came round and they had a snowball fight, then they built a snowman, and a snowgilbert, and a snowcastle.

It was great fun until the Little Princess began to feel
REALLY, REALLY, REALLY COLD.
"Snow is cold!" she sniffed. "I DON'T LIKE SNOW."